for Richard Scarry

FIRST AMERICAN EDITION PUBLISHED IN 2017 BY GECKO PRESS USA,
AN IMPRINT OF GECKO PRESS LTD.

THIS EDITION FIRST PUBLISHED IN 2016 BY GECKO PRESS
PO BOX 9335, MARION SQUARE, WELLINGTON 6141, NEW ZEALAND
INFO@GECKOPRESS.COM

ENGLISH LANGUAGE EDITION © GECKO PRESS LTD 2016

ORIGINAL TITLE: TOUT TOUT SUR LES TOUTOUS
TEXT AND ILLUSTRATIONS BY DOROTHÉE DE MONFREID
© 2015 L'ÉCOLE DES LOISIRS, PARIS

DISTRIBUTED IN THE UNITED STATES AND CANADA BY LERNER PUBLISHING GROUP
WWW.LERNERBOOKS.COM
DISTRIBUTED IN THE UNITED KINGDOM BY BOUNCE SALES AND MARKETING
WWW.BOUNCEMARKETING.CO.UK
DISTRIBUTED IN AUSTRALIA BY SCHOLASTIC AUSTRALIA
WWW.SCHOLASTIC.COM.AU
DISTRIBUTED IN NEW ZEALAND BY UPSTART DISTRIBUTION
WWW.UPSTARTPRESS.CO.NZ

FONT CREATED BY JF REY
TRANSLATED BY LINDA BURGESS
TYPESETTING BY VIDA & LUKE KELLY, NEW ZEALAND
PRINTED IN MALAYSIA

ISBN: 978-1-776570-98-0

FOR MORE CURIOUSLY GOOD BOOKS VISIT GECKOPRESS.COM

Dorothée de Monfreid

A DAY with DOGS

WHAT DO DOGS
DO ALL DAY?

GECKO PRESS

DOGS

SHIH TZU

PYRENEAN SHEPHERD

CHIHUAHUA

ST BERNARD

AFGHAN HOUND

DALMATIAN

NEWFOUNDLAND

BORDER COLLIE

BOXER

LABRADOR

6

AT HOME

ANTENNA

PLAYROOM

TELEVISION

CHEST

BATHRO

BEDROOM

BUNKS

WINDOW   SHUTTER

LOGS

KITCHEN

SHED

TABLE   FRIDGE

BICYCLE

WATERING CAN

ROOF

CHIMNEY

WALL

STAIRS

COMPUTER

LAMP

DRAFTING TABLE

OFFICE

FRONT DOOR

LIVING ROOM

FIREPLACE

ARMCHAIR

RUG

LADDER

DOORMAT

BOAT

9

THE BATHROOM

MIRROR

GLASS

TOWEL RAIL

MEDICINE CABINET

TOOTHBRUSHES

HAIRBRUSH

SINK

TOWEL

TOOTHPASTE

CUPBOARD

BATHROBE

TOILET

TOILET PAPER

CLOTHES

UNDERWEAR

SOCKS

TIGHTS

T-SHIRT

TANK TOP

GLASSES

SHIRT

TROUSERS

JEANS

SKIRTS

OVERALLS

DRESS

NECKLACES

CAP

HAT

HOW DO I LOOK IN THIS DRESS?

BOOTS

SNEAKERS

SHOES

WE'RE GOING TO SCHOOL!

YOU HAVE TO WEAR CLOTHES AT SCHOOL.

WINTER HAT

GLOVES

SCARF

SWEATER

JACKET

RAINCOAT

COAT

IN TOWN

BOW-WOW CAFÉ

PHARMACY

SCHOOL BUS

BUILDING

AT SCHOOL

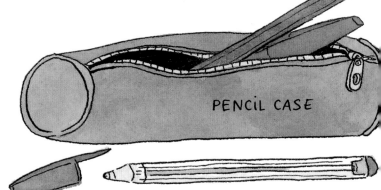

PENCIL CASE

PEN

RULER

SCHOOLBAG

PENCIL

FELT-TIP PEN

SCISSORS

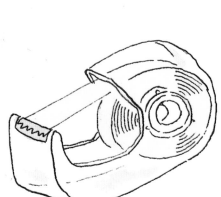

TAPE

GLUE STICK

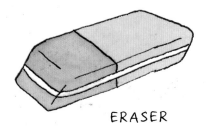

ERASER

NOTEBOOK

NUMBERS

 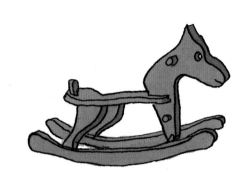 

1 ROCKING HORSE

  BOOF!

2 BALLS

3 BOOKS

4 DOLLS

5 BOWLING PINS

6 SOFT TOYS

7 NESTING DOLLS

8 CANDLES

9 TOY CARS

10 BLOCKS

11 SWEET TREATS

I WANT SOME!

I WANT SOME!

THE ALPHABET

Misha

Toto

Nono

Una

HOP.

THAT'S ME!

Omar

Vera

AND PEDRO!

Popov

Walter

WHEEE!

Quentin

Xavier

TOOT

Raoul

Yardley

Sarah

Zaza

21

ART CLASS

WHITE

BLACK

GRAY

BLACK

WHITE

APRON

PALETTE

PAINTBRUSH

STEPLADDER

ROLLER

SHEET OF PAPER

TUBE OF PAINT

PAINTBOX

PASTELS

SPLASH

INK

23

AT WORK

FISHERMAN

TRUCK DRIVER

BRICKLAYER

PRESIDENT

CLOWN

BAKER

COWGIRL

TEACHER

ILLUSTRATOR

HAIRDRESSER

PILOT

VROOM

DANCER

COOK

BE BOP A LULA YEAH YEAH

SINGER

SIT!

LION TAMER

SAY AH.

AAH.

VET

WRITER

FIREFIGHTER

MUSICIAN

25

SPORTS

WARM-UP

RUNNING

WEIGHT LIFTING

TENNIS

JUDO

FOOTBALL...OR SOCCER!

AT THE DOCTOR

NURSE

CART

MEDICATION 200MG
MEDICATION 900MG

PILL

TAPE

SLURP.

MEDICINE

STETHOSCOPE

BAND-AID

THERMOMETER

SYRINGE

TABLET

PAW CREAM
200ml

OINTMENT

RASH

HONK

HANDKERCHIEF

COLD

I ALWAYS WANTED CRUTCHES.

CAST

BROKEN LEG

OUCH.

BANDAGE

WOUND

IN THE COUNTRY

SKY

SUN

FOREST

LIGHTHOUSE

MEADOW

TREE

FARM

FENCE

31

THE FARM

COW

FARMHOUSE

HUTCH

CLOTHESLINE

RA

MILK CAN

RAKE

PIG

WHEELBARROW

PIGSTY

ZZZ

WEATHERVANE

TRACTOR

SOIL

APPLE TREE

STABLE

DONKEY

HORSE

CART

PONY

GOAT

ROOSTER

LAMB

SHEEP

CHICKS

HENS

GRAIN

DUCK

HENHOUSE

KLINGS

POND

33

ANIMALS

SPARROW

PIGEON

in town

CAT

GOLDFISH

HAMSTER

HARE

BLUETIT

CROAK.

FROG

BEE

SPIDER

SNAIL

SALAMANDER

TORTOISE

in the country

FLOWERS

POPPY

DAISY

TULIP

ROSE

DANDELION

BUTTERCUP

SUNFLOWER

SUNFLOWER SEED

INSECTS

LADYBUG

ANT

BUTTERFLY

WASP

FLY

OUCH.

BEETLE

CATERPILLAR

BZZZ

MOSQUITO

GRASSHOPPER

CICADA

STAG BEETLE

DRAGONFLY

THE SEA

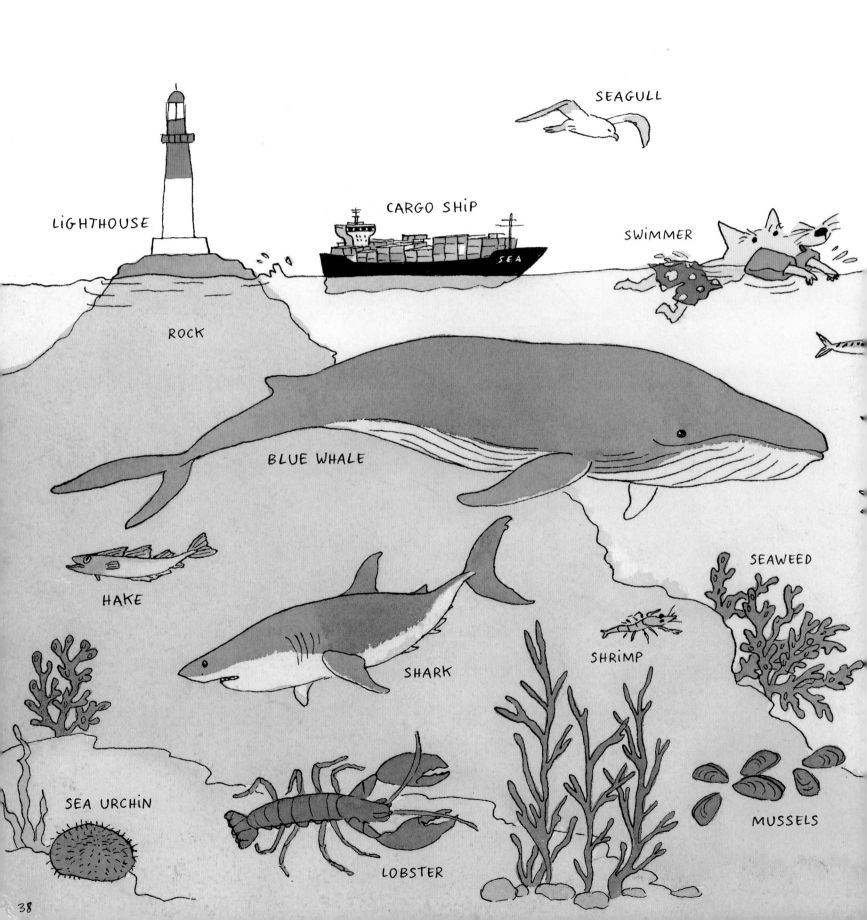

LIGHTHOUSE

ROCK

CARGO SHIP

SEA

SEAGULL

SWIMMER

BLUE WHALE

HAKE

SHARK

SEAWEED

SHRIMP

SEA URCHIN

LOBSTER

MUSSELS

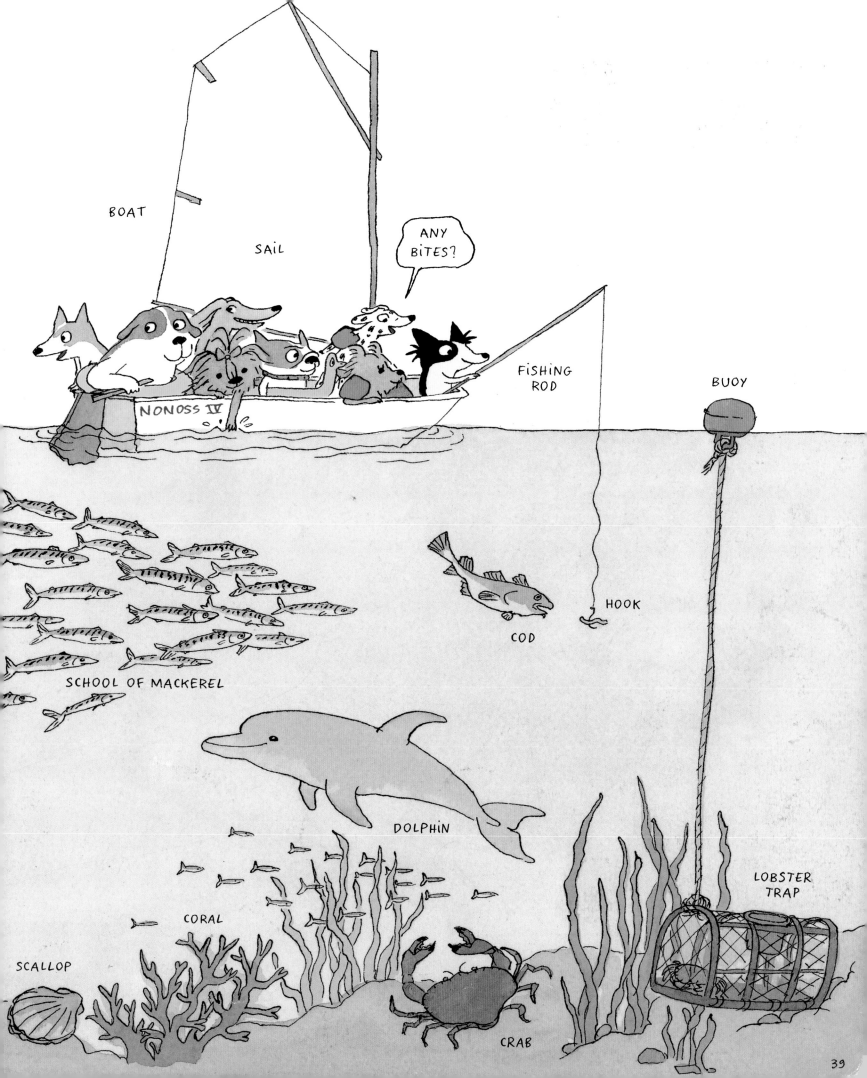

THE FOREST

NEST

BIRCH TREES

FERNS

CHESTNUTS

KNIFE

STRING

BACKPACK

HUT

OAK TREE

ACORN

THE MOUNTAIN

PINE TREES

SKI TOW

MONOSKI

PISTE 3

SNOWBALLS

SNOW BOOTS

SNOWMAN

SEASONS

spring

summer

A BIRTHDAY PARTY

PIÑATA

STREAMER

PRESENTS

TREATS

VEHICLES

TRAIN

BUS

SPORTS CAR

MOTORSCOOTER

BICYCLE

PLANE

HELICOPTER

TRUCK

VAN

CARAVAN

CAR

MOTORCYCLE

SCOOTER

SKATEBOARD

ROLLERSKATES

THE SUPERMARKET

AISLE

DAIRY PRODUCTS

YOGURT

MILK

CHEESE

EGGS

HOT DOGS

TEA

COFFEE

FLOUR

SUGAR

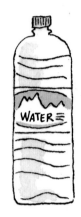

MINERAL
WATER

FRUIT JUICE

BREAD

BUTTER

RECEIPT

CASHIER

CASH
REGISTER

GROCERIES

CONVEYOR
BELT

BASKET

CREDIT
CARD

OH DEAR,
THAT WAS
EXPENSIVE.

SHOPPING BAG

VEGETABLES

WHO WANTS ONE?

POTATO

CORN

RADISH

TOMATO

CARROT

GRATED CARROT

HMM...

LETTUCE

ARTICHOKE

PEPPER

ZUCCHINI

ONION

PEAS

LEEK

GREEN BEAN

FRUIT

BANANA

YUM!

ORANGE JUICE

ORANGE

APRICOT

LEMON

TRAWBERRY

RASPBERRY

CHERRIES

PINEAPPLE

APPLE

PEAR

SLURP.

MELON

SEEDS

RED CURRANTS

BLACKBERRY

GRAPES

THE KITCHEN

LIGHT

CLOCK

WOODEN SPOONS

BLENDER

STEAM

KETTLE

SPON...

LADLE

SINK

POTS

DRAWER

STOVE

CUPBOARD

TOWEL

OVEN

SALAMI

KNIFE

SALT SHAKER

CUTTING BOARD

PEPPER GRINDER

RECIPE BOOK

APPLE PIE

DINNERTIME

MUSIC

ADOOBADAAOPPWAA
AKIAKIAA
ADOKK
KKcRRR

RADIO

TOOM TOOM TOOM

TOOM TOOM TOOM

TING

TRIANGLE

ziiiiiuiuuu
ziiuuu
ZUuiriu

VIOLIN

DOUBLE BASS

ziooooN
ZiOOON
ZiOOoN

BOW

CELLO

DZiiiAONN
WAiiiiOOi
DZiiiNG
ROAARR

ELECTRIC GUITAR

WEEOOUUU WEEEOO

MUSICAL SAW

WAAMP
WAAMP
WAAMP WAAMMP

TROMBONE

TING TIKI TING

BANJO

GLING GLING BELING GLING

GUITAR

MUSIC STAND

WAPADA WAPDOUAA WAPDAM BILAP

SONG

BOOM TISH

PAF BLANG

SBAM BALAM TCHING

TSS TSSS

DRUM KIT

TCHAP TCHAP TCHAP

TAMBOURINE

DIGILING DING DILING DILING DZING DILING DING

DILING DZING DIGILING

UKULELE

ZWAAN WAAMP WAA ZWAA WAAM

POOON POOON Piiin

CLARINET

TRUMPET

ZAZAZOON ZOONN ZAZON

SAXOPHONE

AVOON VOON OOON

VOOOON

HARMONICA

CRRitch RROCKA CRRr

TURNTABLE

PLING PLING PLONG

PLING PLONG

PIANO

59

NIGHT